EVERYMAN'S LIBRARY

EVERYMAN,
I WILL GO WITH THEE,
AND BE THY GUIDE,
IN THY MOST NEED
TO GO BY THY SIDE

ANTHONY TROLLOPE

BARCHESTER TOWERS

WITH AN INTRODUCTION
BY VICTORIA GLENDINNING

EVERYMAN'S LIBRARY
Alfred A. Knopf New York London Toronto

THIS IS A BORZOI BOOK
PUBLISHED BY ALFRED A. KNOPF

First included in Everyman's Library, 1906
Introduction Copyright © 1992 by Victoria Glendinning
Bibliography and Chronology Copyright © 1992 by Everyman's Library
Printed from the Shakespeare Head edition, 1929, by kind
permission of Basil Blackwell Ltd.

US website: www.randomhouse.com/everymans

ISBN: 978-0-679-40587-0 (US)
978-1-85715-057-5 (UK)

A CIP catalogue reference for this book is available from the
British Library

Library of Congress Cataloging-in-Publication Data
Trollope, Anthony, 1815–1882.
Barchester Towers / Anthony Trollope.
p. cm.—(Everyman's library)
ISBN 978-0-679-40587-0
I. Title. II. Series Everyman's library (Alfred A. Knopf)
PR5684.B3 1992   91-53197
823'.8—dc20   CIP

Printed and bound in Germany by GGP Media GmbH, Pössneck

BARCHESTER TOWERS